The story of Abraham retold simply and
delightfully illustrated for young readers.

Note to parents and teachers
*The complex stories of the patriarch Abraham are to be found in
Genesis, chapters 12-25. This simplified account of them
concentrates on God's promises to Abraham, and on Abraham's
deep faith in God.*

British Library Cataloguing in Publication Data
Hately, David
    Abraham.
    1. Bible. O.T. Genesis. Abraham – Stories for children
    I. Title   II. Langton, Roger
    III. [Bible, O.T. Genesis. *English. Selections. 1988*]
    IV. Series
    222'.110924
    ISBN 0-7214-1110-X

First edition
Published by Ladybird Books Ltd Loughborough Leicestershire UK
Ladybird Books Inc Auburn Maine 04210 USA
© LADYBIRD BOOKS LTD MCMLXXXVIII
Printed in England

Abraham

written by David Hately
illustrated by Roger Langton

Ladybird Books

Slowly the little band of travellers crossed the desert. During the day it was hot and dusty; at night it was bitterly cold. There wasn't much food, and water was difficult to find.

The men were angry because their leader, whose name was Abraham, had made them set out on this terrible journey. The women were afraid of the dangers. The children were tired and hungry, and didn't know why they had left home.

They all said it was Abraham's fault.

4

But Abraham wasn't angry, or afraid or tired, for God had asked him to make the long and dangerous journey.

'I want you to leave your own country,' God had told him. 'Leave your father's house and go to a land that I will show you. I am going to make you the father of a great nation.

Your name will be famous.'

So Abraham and his wife, Sarah, took everything they owned and set out with their followers for the new land that God had promised them.

Abraham trusted God. He was sure that one day they would all reach the promised land that God had spoken of.

And God kept his word. For after many years of wandering, Abraham reached Canaan, where he and his people settled down to live. It was a fertile land, and they grew rich there.

Among Abraham's followers was his nephew, whose name was Lot. Now the men who looked after Lot's animals were always quarrelling with Abraham's own herdsmen.

Time after time, fighting would break out between them. Finally, Abraham decided to put a stop to it.

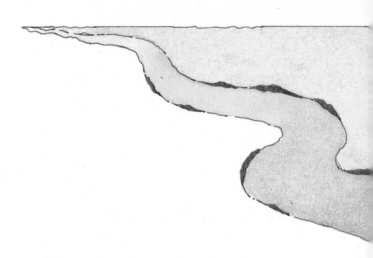

Abraham sent for Lot. 'We shouldn't argue among ourselves,' he told his nephew. 'We all belong to the same family.'

Then Abraham took Lot up on to some high ground, and together they looked at the land that spread out below.

'Look to the east,' said Abraham. 'Then look to the west. Choose which side of the land you want and take it. I'll be satisfied with the rest.'

Lot could hardly believe his ears. For the land to the east was a fertile plain, watered by the River Jordan. It was much richer than the land that lay to the west.

Lot took his men and their herds into the rich eastern plains. But Abraham went westward. He and his followers settled at a sacred place called Mamre, near the town of Hebron.

After Lot had gone, God made Abraham another promise. 'Wherever you look,' he said, 'whether north, south, east or west, the land you see will one day belong to your children.'

But Abraham was puzzled. He and Sarah had no children, so how could God keep his promise?

*   *   *

One day, as Sarah sat in her tent, keeping cool out of the hot desert sun, she heard Abraham talking to three strangers. She had no idea who they were or where they had come from.

Suddenly, Abraham came hurrying to the tent and asked her to get a big meal ready for their guests.

'These people must be important!'
Sarah said to herself as she hurried
off to prepare the food.

When the meal was ready,
Abraham laid it all out under the
shade of a tree. But Sarah went back
to the tent so that she could overhear
what the visitors were saying to
Abraham.

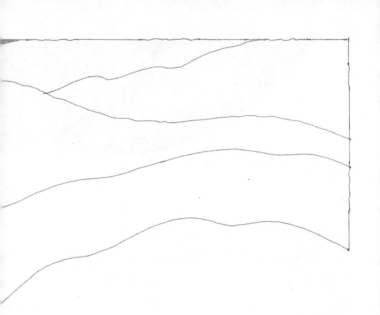

Abraham watched carefully as the strangers ate and drank. He knew that they were the messengers of God.

One of them asked where Sarah was. 'She is inside the tent,' answered Abraham.

'About this time next year,' the stranger said, 'I will visit you again. For by then your wife will have a son.'

Sarah burst out laughing. The idea of it! She knew that she was much too old to have a child!

Then one of the strangers called out to her. 'Sarah, why did you laugh?' he asked.

'Me? Laugh?' Sarah called back nervously. 'I didn't laugh.'

'Oh, but you did!' replied the stranger. 'Do you think it is impossible for God to send you a child?'

*   *   *

And before the next spring, Sarah gave birth to a child, just as the stranger had said she would.

It was a baby boy, and Abraham and Sarah named him Isaac, which means 'laughter'.

As Sarah looked down at her child, she said, 'Now God has really given me something to laugh and sing about! Everyone who hears the story of my baby will share my happiness.'

And Isaac grew up to be the apple of Abraham's eye.

*   *   *

Abraham had always done whatever God had asked of him. But now God wanted to put Abraham's faith to a final test. So he called out to Abraham.

'Yes, Lord?' answered Abraham. 'Here I am!'

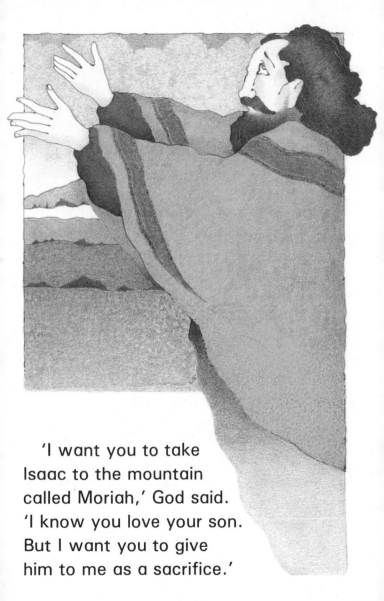

'I want you to take
Isaac to the mountain
called Moriah,' God said.
'I know you love your son.
But I want you to give
him to me as a sacrifice.'

Abraham was horrified. He could not believe what God had asked him to do.

Now when Abraham's people offered a sacrifice to God, they took an animal and killed it. The flesh was then burned upon an altar, so that its sweet scent would go up to God.

But God was not asking Abraham to kill an animal. He was asking for Abraham's son, Isaac.

Abraham was filled with grief. He didn't know what to do.

Abraham tried to shut his ears to God's voice, but he couldn't do it.

So, early next morning, he saddled one of the donkeys. Then he went to chop some wood for a fire.

Next he fetched a sharp knife, and when everything was ready he sent for Isaac.

The boy was delighted to learn that he was going on a journey with his father.

It was a long journey, but on the third day they could see the mountain in the distance.

When they reached the foot of the mountain, Abraham unloaded the wood from the donkey's back and tied it to Isaac's back. He took the knife, and the flint to start a fire, and they began to climb.

'Father!' said Isaac. 'You've got the knife. You've got a flint for the fire. I'm carrying the wood. But you've forgotten to bring a lamb for the sacrifice!' Isaac laughed as he spoke.

'God will provide the sacrifice,' his father answered quietly. And the two of them went on together until they reached the mountain top.

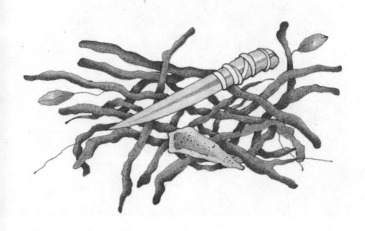

At the top of the mountain, Abraham and Isaac built an altar with some stones. Then they arranged the firewood on it.

When everything was ready Abraham took hold of his son and bound him hand and foot. He lifted Isaac in his arms and placed him on the altar.

But God was watching.

As Abraham raised the knife, God called out to him, 'Abraham! Abraham!'

'I'm here, Lord!' answered Abraham.

'Do not harm the boy,' God said.
'You have proved how much you trust
me. You were even willing to give me
your son.'

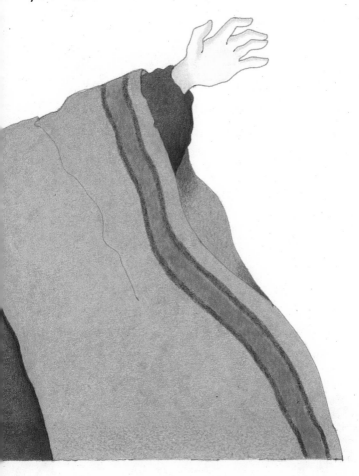

As Abraham cut the ropes from Isaac's hands and feet, tears of joy ran down his cheeks. His son was going to live!

Then Abraham saw a ram, caught by its horns in a bush that grew nearby. So he took the ram and offered it to God instead of his son, Isaac.

God had provided the sacrifice, after all.

45

Before setting off home, Abraham looked round at the mountain called Moriah and gave it a new name. The name he chose means 'God provides'.

Even today there is a saying among
people who know the mountains:
*When you are on the mountain, it is
God who provides.*

God never again put Abraham's
faith to the test, and Abraham lived
peacefully for the rest of his life. In
his old age he had plenty of time to
think about God's promise — that he
would be the father of a great nation.

Abraham realised that he would not
live to see it for himself. God's
promise would come true through
Isaac, Abraham's son.

Sarah did not live to see her son's wedding. Isaac married a beautiful girl called Rebecca, who came from Abraham's own people in the country he had left behind so long ago.

But Abraham lived to a good old age, and Isaac always took care of him. When Abraham died, he was buried next to his wife near to his home at Mamre.